D1613078

THIS BLOOMSBURY BOOK

BELONGS TO

....

For Mum, Dad,
Chris and Claire,
my inspiration.

BLOOMSBURY
CHILDREN'S
BOOKS

First published in Great Britain in 2005 by Bloomsbury Publishing Plc
38 Soho Square, London, W1D 3HB

Text and illustrations copyright © Stephen Waterhouse 2005
The moral right of the author/illustrator has been asserted

A CIP catalogue record of this book is available from the British Library

ISBN 0 7475 7576 2

Printed in China

1 3 5 7 9 10 8 6 4 2

All papers used by Bloomsbury Publishing are natural, recyclable products
made from wood grown in well-managed forests. The manufacturing processes
conform to the environmental regulations of the country of origin.

GET BUSY, DAD'S BACK!

Stephen Waterhouse

BLOOMSBURY
CHILDREN'S
BOOKS

One morning in the penguin igloo,
Mum was quietly knitting.

Pip, Pilly, Peni and Poy were playing, painting and reading. Suddenly they heard footsteps coming towards the front door.

The door burst open and there was Dad, back from his travels!

Mum and the baby penguins were so pleased to see him.

Dad had been away for a long time.

They had missed him and couldn't wait to have a big hug.

They rolled out Dad's map of the world so that he could show them where he had travelled.

Start here

'I started my journey here, from the South Pole.' said Dad.

MAP OF

Dad pointed out all the wonderful and exciting countries he had been to.

'Here you are, Pip, look what I got for you when I visited Sydney in AUSTRALIA.'

Little Pip opened his presents. 'I painted Sydney Harbour because I really love the colour of the water and all the small boats,' said Dad.

The Sydney Opera House

'Here you are, Pilly, look what
I got for you from Agra in INDIA.'

Pilly opened her presents. 'I painted the Taj Mahal because the decoration and detail are beautiful,' said Dad.

The Sydney Opera House

The Taj Mahal

'Here you are, Peni, look what I got
for you from Moscow in RUSSIA.'

Peni opened her presents. 'I painted the
Church of St Basil because the colours
on the rooftops are just magical,' said Dad.

'Here you are, Poy, look what I got for you when I visited New York City in AMERICA.'

Poy opened his presents. 'I painted the Empire State Building because it is so tall. I went right to the top and everything looked tiny down below,' said Dad.

'Here you are, Mum, look what I got
for you from Paris in FRANCE.'

Mum opened her presents. 'I painted the Eiffel Tower because it is such an interesting shape,' said Dad.

And then they made a *fun* city of their own!

The Empire
State Building

The
Taj Mahal

They used cardboard and lots of paint.

The Eiffel Tower

The Church of St Basil

The Sydney Opera House

Then after listening to more of Dad's stories, they all fell fast asleep and dreamt of their own adventures!

'Happy Dreaming, Penguins!'

The Sydney Opera House

The Taj Mahal

The Church of St Basil

The Empire State Building

The Eiffel Tower

The Sydney Opera House

The Taj Mahal

The Church of St Basil

The Empire State Building

The Eiffel Tower

Enjoy more great picture books from Stephen Waterhouse ...

Get Busy This Christmas!
Stephen Waterhouse

Get Busy This Summer!
Stephen Waterhouse

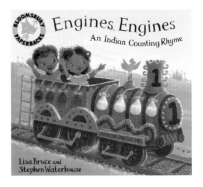

Engines, Engines
Lisa Bruce & Stephen Waterhouse

All now available in paperback